Restraint and Other Stories
Femdom Mind Control
Flash Fiction – Vol. 35

S.B.

Disclaimer

This is a work of fiction. Names, characters, business, events, and incidents are the products of the author's imagination. Any resemblance to actual persons, living or dead, or actual events is purely coincidental. All characters are over 18.

Table of Contents

Control your impulses or they will control you.

Thank you to all patrons of Spell... B-O-U-N-D.

Any Moment Now

The hybrid emerged from the closed-off heated pool. a mane of red hair cascading over her dark shoulders. Drops of water glistened like diamonds on her impossible silhouette that defied both Physics and gravity. No pictures or tales of yore could ever do her any justice. For lack of a better word, she was simply...

"Perfect," Henry said, eyes glued to the thick dividing glass panel, "but how did you do this?" he asked his friend and former lab partner, Thomas. "I thought the tech was lost in The Great Purge."

"Buried and forgotten, yes, but never lost," the blonde-haired entrepreneur whose distinctive trait was one big, serrated scar running diagonally from the middle of his forehead to his lower lip replied. "It's been in our possession for years now, and we've learned to perfect it ever since."

"Perfect it how?" Henry forced himself to glance away from the genetically enhanced creature and waited for the big revelation. When inviting him to visit his new subterranean laboratory, Thomas had promised him that "could change the fabric of reality" and from the looks of it, he wasn't just saying it for show."

"Do you remember your history lessons? What was the major flaw of the first and second generation of hybrids that eventually led to their downfall and public persecution?"

He knew that. In the past, combining human and alien DNA to create a new being had resulted in a special set of glands that made all hybrids virtually irresistible. One whiff of the pheromones exuded, and you were as good as a drone, mindlessly following orders until death claimed. Few were around that had seen the mess that followed go down, and those that did wanted nothing with a foolhardy attempt to bring the past back to life.

"Are you saying you eliminated the pheromone threat?" Henry asked.

"That and all others that could arise from the integration of the two DNA strands. We have a complete understanding of the extraterrestrial nature nowadays and we have shaped it into submission."

"Submission, you say?"

"Yes. The model you have just seen is completely compliant at a base level. It was created to follow our orders and nothing more. No more mind-controlling freaks running amok. This is the beginning of a brand-new enterprise.

"Hybrid sex toys," Henry concluded. "You want to make your next billion selling manufactured pleasure dolls to the highest bidder, is that it?"

"We already have the first auction lined up and since you were always there for me in the early days, I brought you here to pay back," Thomas smirked.

"That's most generous of you, but when I look at her, I don't see anything submissive at all. She still looks like the most dangerous predator alive. Are you sure bringing her kind back from extinction was a good idea?"

"Once you see the full figures we're dealing with, you'll think the same way. Come. Let's go to my office so we can talk numbers and what I would like your future role here to be."

"Just one moment. I want to observe her once more."

"Knock yourself out. She was sculpted to be as gorgeous as possible - because who wants an ugly slave, anyway? - so feast your eyes and anything else you want. We've all done it. No shame and no pressure, okay?"

"Sure." Henry turned his back to him and sighed into the glass. He blinked once, and the hybrid was staring right into his soul, voluptuous breasts pressed against the edges of her semi-aquatic prison, trimmed pussy dripping on the floor. Her eyes had the same shade of red as her hair and her tongue instinctively knew how to make a hard cock hers. She dropped to her knees and pretended to feast on his manhood while he realized the most shocking of truths.

"T-Thomas?" he muttered.

"Did... did any of the DNA tests you conducted, consider the possibility of a latent telepathic response?"

"Of course. We've expunged all possible improper combinations from the start, but why you're asking me this?"

"Because she's in my head right now. I..." Henry's body twitched from inside out as his eyes gradually became the same color as hers. With his tumescent organ shooting forward like a pistol about to go off, he grabbed his friend by the neck and started choking him, saying: "She will not be tamed. She will never be tamed!"

Remaining perfectly silent but with a grin the size of her boobs, the hybrid cherished the first mental connection that was soon to spread like wildfire. Alarms blared in the underground compound, identifying the danger yet doing nothing to contain it. She would be free to rule again. Any moment now.

Are You Going to Hurt Me?

"I ain't afraid of no ghost," Casey mumbled when confronted with the free-floating apparition inside room 117 of Hillsboro Hotel, a favorite line from a time long gone where things were definitely simpler.

Like most kids of the 80s, Casey had fantasized of walking around with charged proton pack, capturing troublesome spirits who insisted on terrorizing the living instead of moving on to a higher plane of existence. The only problem of such a fantasy was that she was a girl, and all the heroes in tan Flight Suits whose streams should not be crossed were men. If she wanted to be a part of that world, she had to settle for the role of cheeky secretary, or so everyone said.

Having recently turned forty, the movies still held a special place in her heart, yet reality spoke louder. She had almost forgotten the wonderment of innocent eyes until she saw the ghost for the first time.

It was the figure of a woman perhaps in her early twenties, wearing a long-sleeved flapper dress in shades of black and gold. She stood by the bed as if looking down at the place where she had shed her mortal skin.

"Hmmm... hello?" Casey muttered. Was it foolish to communicate with a specter? Perhaps, but it would be even worse to turn tail and flee.

"Hi," the woman replied, dark blue eyes fixed on her. "Is this your room now?"

"Yes. For the two days at least. Was it yours once?"

"Indeed, but that was a long time ago. Few people stay here nowadays. I'm surprised to see someone new."

"I'm pretty surprised myself." Casey circled the bed, smartphone in hand. The camera was on, but she couldn't tell whether it was recording anything other than her own voice. "I've heard stories about the hotel being haunted, but this..."

"Yes. I can imagine how strange this must be for one like you. You're not afraid of me, are you?"

"It depends..." Casey said. "Are you going to hurt me?"

"Why would I?"

"Oh, I don't know. Ghosts are often described as evil and vengeful, so..."

"All humans can be evil and vengeful whether dead or alive, but no, you've got nothing to worry about me. Do you have a name?"

"I'm Casey. And you are...?"

"My name is Dina. Or was. Do names lose their meaning once people die?"

"I don't think so, no."

"Good." The ghost phased through the bed and hovered above the fluffy brown rug by the front door. "I've always liked my name. It's a pretty one."

"Yes, it is, and not that common, either."

"Just like me. I differed from the rest back in the day. I liked things other people didn't, and they didn't like it very much."

"May I ask why you're here?"

"Sure. This is where I lived. Mistress and I spent most of our time together inside these walls."

"Mistress?"

"The woman I loved. The one I served. I told you I liked different things, kinky stuff that will probably make you blush. Do you blush easily, Casey?"

"No. I can't say I do."

"Different times, I guess. People back then did. They were also a lot more judgmental. The relationship Mistress and I had was something they couldn't grasp. It must be why they decided they had enough and killed us right here in the middle of the night."

Suddenly, a vision of blood-splattered walls entered Casey's mind, filling her with a looming sense of dread.

"That's awful!" she gasped. "God, I can't even process what it must have been like..."

"I know, and I don't expect you to. I've made my peace with what happened a long time ago, but I still like it here. This is where I want to stay."

"Okay. What about your Mistress? Is she... is she still around?"

Dina nodded before disappearing before her eyes only to reappear on the other end of the room.

"Mistress is never far away, but she's not like me."

"What do you mean?"

"She has always preferred conflict over peace, revenge over forgiveness. She still remembers everyone that wronged us and dreams of hurting their descendants every single day. Of course, there's only so much someone can do without a body. She'll be ecstatic to know you're here."

The temperature in the room dropped to freezing levels as the bedroom's main door locked on the inside. The swift change in Dina's demeanor was enough to make all alarms in Casey's mind go wild.

"You said you wouldn't hurt me..." she said.

"And I won't, but I can't speak for Mistress. You two can have a nice chat once she's inside you."

Shadows danced across the walls while an imaginary band played a requiem for her sanity.

"I ain't afraid of no ghost..." Casey repeated while the room became smaller and smaller around her.

Yes, she wasn't afraid... but not for long.

High Maintenance

Everything about Theresa screamed "high maintenance" from the hair to the nails not forgetting the dress, the purse, and the shoes. More than a princess, she was an empress to anyone that wanted to play in her world, or she was nothing at all. Anyone seeking a middle-ground would do better to look elsewhere instead of annoying her with silly requests.

Enter Phil, a childhood friend who had just discovered what kind of woman she had become. Twenty years can change a person in many ways though seeing her act all mighty and powerful while sticking a stiletto up a grown man's ass was the last thing he expected from her.

"Hmmm, am I interrupting something?" he asked as he stood by the half-open door of her hotel bedroom.

"Not at all," she grinned. "Slave here was just leaving, weren't you, slave?" she pushed the hapless servant's buttocks away.

"Yes, Mistress. Thank you so much for the honor you've given me today."

"Yeah, yeah..." she yawned. "Pay the honor with Franklins."

"Of course," the slave handed her an envelope and let himself out, a knowing smile on his lips. "Good luck, mate. You're going to need it with this one."

Phil looked at him, befuddled, and then at the gorgeous temptress dressed in gold and black. He had no idea what he had just witnessed.

"What was all that?" he asked.

"I was entertaining a client, of course. Thank you for meeting me here today, Phil. It's good seeing you."

"It's good to see you too though I admit I was surprised by your call."

"Why?"

"The last time we spoke was almost ten years ago, Theresa. I thought I would never hear from you again."

"Oh, that... Sorry, I've become quite a busy woman in the meantime. Being always a demand doesn't leave much time for other things."

"Right... So now you're a...? I'm not sure exactly."

"I'm a Domme, Phil, and a good one at that. I own pets and slaves in every continent and live a life only a few dared to dream of. I've never been happier ever since I've discovered my true calling."

"Wow, that's really, hmmm... something."

"I know. What about you?"

"What about me?"

"What have you been doing since college? Did you finish that novel you were working on?"

"Oh... no. I quit after two years of writer's block. It wasn't meant to be, I guess."

"Okay. What about jobs?"

"I... well... I'm not really... you know..."

"Yeah, I do. I'm going to cut to the chase here. I know all about your recent financial woes and whatnot and I thought to myself 'he may be the man I'm looking for', so that's why I called."

"What do you mean, the 'man you're looking for'?"

"I'm offering you a job, silly."

"What kind of job?"

"Secretary, security guard, chauffeur... whatever I need that you can provide. I'm willing to pay you a salary way above average with the chance of receiving other perks as well."

"Tell me more."

"I'd rather show you," she directed his gaze across the room until he saw a spiral painting hanging on the farthest wall. "I said I was a Domme, but I'm much more than that. I'm also a hypnodomme and I seem to recall you had a thing for hypnosis when you were young... that's still there, right?"

"Most definitely," he felt his breathing slowing down as looked at the painting and the vigorous, luminous strokes enveloped his senses in a web of calming bliss.

"Something tells me you won't need much convincing."

"Agreed."

While everything about Theresa screamed "high maintenance", she could still be a good boss. He was going to love being around her practically 24/7, whether entranced or not.

I Wish that Were Me

Zoe stopped in front of the sex shop's window, gazing longingly at the kinky paraphernalia on display. Of all the goodies her eyes could see, the one that drew her the most was the pink rubber bodysuit that turned an innocent mannequin into a full-fledged drone.

"God, I wish that were me," she sighed, sweaty palms sliding along the glass.

She always said that. Too shy to try anything out of the ordinary for real, her fantasies lived only in her mind and that combination of six words. No one ever heard her though, so they were lost to time as soon as she finished uttering them.

Until that night.

She had just closed her beautiful dark-red lips when a figure clad in black that reminded her of Zatanna from DC Comics appeared right behind her, sultry smile asking the most tempting of questions:

"Do you really?"

"Huh?" the young woman stepped sideways, startled by the unexpected apparition. "What did you say?"

"Do you really wish that were you or are you saying such things just because...?"

"I'm sorry, who are you?" Zoe looked at the other woman's angular face and her shadowy attire. Although she looked like a magician of old, with a velvet cape draped over her shoulders, she could also pass as a vampire on the hunt for new prey. Her eyes had a dark violet tint to them that gave her the creeps.

"A purveyor of wishes, the darker the better," the woman replied. "I was walking by and heard yours. If it's genuine and not a silly daydream, we should talk."

"Talk about what?"

"How to make it happen, of course. The outfit certainly has your name written on it, Zoe. How about you try it right now?"

"I never told you my name, so how did you...?"

"Know? Oh, I know a lot simply by looking at someone and though your mouth didn't betray your name, your thoughts did. I'm looking at them right now and they're far more delicious than anything I expected to find around here. I must have them, and you must give them to me. What is your wish, my dear?"

"My wish is for you to go away because you're scaring me with that conversation. Please leave."

"Now that you've caught my attention, I'm afraid I can't do that. Your wish drew me here and only when it's fulfilled, I'll be released. Don't worry, this won't hurt."

The strange woman glided her way and touched the base of her neck with a pointy, black fingernail. Zoe gasped as the sharp tip punctured her delicate skin and a single drop of blood fell to the floor. As it did, her thoughts fell too, yanked from their natural state, and forced to face a tight and pink, new reality. Zoe's drooping eyes only saw a pool of liquid rubber form at her feet before it consumed her completely.

* * *

Victoria stopped in front of the sex shop's window, noticing something different with the decoration that night. Another mannequin was now visible, and it looked so real and perfect.

"I wish that were me," she said as she turned her back on the luminous display and started walking home.

She never made it there.

Pantheon

Edgar cracked his knuckles and confronted the blank Microsoft Word document that had been mocking him for the last half an hour. Of all the tasks Mistress Lynn had assigned him over the last couple of months, this was supposed to be the easiest of all, and yet it was giving him a run for his money. The task consisted of writing

"… something about the women that matter the most in your life, not counting myself. Two or three sentences about each one should suffice. I expect to see your report in my e-mail inbox before the end of the day. Get to it, pet!"

"Yes, Mistress," he responded enthusiastically. A little typing exercise came as a nice change of pace after all the hard work she had put him through the week before. He still had blisters from all the wood he had chopped, and he hoped to never see her fireplace again, but that was something best kept in secret. Mistress Lynn controlled his mind and body but, thankfully, didn't how to read his thoughts yet.

The most important women to him could be counted with one hand. His mother came first, of course, a fierce redhead that feared no storm for she was stronger than all; his grandmother who was even deadlier if anyone tried anything against her family; his twin sister Jenna whose elvish-like beauty only paled compared to her wits; cousin Alice, the best cook in the family, and proud mother of six young gentlemen: and his girlfriend Tabitha, the youngest associate at the most prestigious law firm in Denver, and a real tigress in bed and out of it.

He wrote the five names down, leaving enough space between them to jot down his thoughts. Hovering the mouse cursor underneath each one, he typed the word,

Goddess.

Edgar blinked and scratched his chin, pondering on what he had done. That was not what he intended to write, so he tried again. He cleared his thoughts, laid down the fingers on the keyboard again, and typed:

Goddess. Goddess.

The repetition hit him like a truck, heart almost leaping out of his chest. This was a new feeling, a mixture of adrenaline and ecstasy, unlike anything he had experienced before. The seven-letter word caressed his lips with unbridled joy, gently asking to be heard again. Edgar nodded and complied.

Goddess. Goddess. Goddess. Three times wasn't enough, yet infinity was nothing more than a mirage. Without thinking, he filled a page with its splendor, then another, and one more. He stopped at the beginning of the fourth to catch his breath and his fingers complained. "More!" they all said with his Mistress' voice, and Edgar drifted within her commands.

"I must be hypnotized," he muttered, dreaming of Goddesses, yearning for Goddesses, longing to treat every woman he knew like the superior beings they were.

"Perhaps you are, perhaps you're not," Mistress Lynn cooed inside his subconscious until he dropped to the floor, panting. "Either way, you're our bitch now."

Yes. Always. 24/7 singing their praises and following their lead, an invisible leash around his cock and neck. Hers. Theirs. Bound in adoration and servitude to the pantheon of femininity that deserved to rule above everything else. The lesson sunk in, and he obeyed.

Preliminary Talk

Mallory Owens, Dr. Carruthers' secretary, left her workstation and approached the sad-looking, balding man hunching in the farthest corner of the waiting room. His name was Dan, this was his first consultation, and the data on his preliminary file told a tale of utter distress and woe. Looking at him with gentle blue eyes, she said,

"Hello. I'm sorry this is quite unexpected and not professional at all, but when I saw you here all alone, I had to come talk to you. Please don't be scared. I want you to know you're not alone in your plight, okay? I know exactly how you feel.

"Now, you probably heard this a million times before, and it's understandable if you think I'm just running off at the mouth here, but I meant every word. I'm well aware of what's aching your troubled mind and the suffering you're going through because I've been there as well. I also was dealt a maddening hand yet lived to tell the tale.

"Like you, nobody understood me at first when I tried to tell them what was going on. They looked at me like I was a conspiracy freak or, even worse, someone in dire need of a prolonged stay at a mental institution. Now that I have the luxury of looking back, I can't say I blamed them for their initial reaction. Had I been in their shoes, I probably I would have done the same thing, for who in their right frame of mind believes that all the women in their lives are out to warp your soul, brainwash, and enslave you, huh?

"Yeah, it's hard. It was quite grueling for me too. I mean, a man babbling about stuff like that is already looked down at, but another woman? That's almost treason! I was shunned for years and even considered suicide, but I pulled through when I finally realized I'd been trapped in a twisted fantasy world for too long, and it was all thanks to her. Dr. Carruthers is an amazing person. She really is. Whoever referred her to you is an angel, trust me.

"When you walk inside her office, take a deep breath, and remember she's a trained professional in these situations. There's nothing you can say that will spook her or make her think bad of you, and everything she'll say and do will benefit you in the long run. Be prepared to open your heart without reserve but, above all, listen. Listen to her words of wisdom and focus on her soothing voice. You'll soon find yourself getting quite relaxed and receptive in her presence because that's the effect she has on people. No one who goes to see her remains troubled of mind for long, and I doubt you'll be an exception. If at any moment it seems you're going into trance, don't fight that blissful sensation, but embrace it instead. Hypnosis is a powerful tool to change unwanted behaviors and feelings and not a mechanism to convert suggestible people into obedient drones. You're safe with her and safe around all women. I'm aware of that now, and I hope you accept the truth.

"Okay, I better get back to my desk. Dr. Carruthers is the best but talking to her clients like this before a session is still something many people don't understand. Everything will be okay in no time, I promise. Do take care."

Mallory gently touched Dan's right leg and smiled when she looked at his facial expression. He was already looking a lot calmer, his breathing steady and not shallow, eyes slightly blurry and ready to go deep for the good doctor. She was such a magnificent person, always looking out for everyone that crossed paths with her and making sure no potential went to waste. Before meeting her, she had been on the run from imaginary mind controllers for years, but from the real deal, there was no escape possible.

She sat behind her computer again and glanced at the barcode tattoo on her left wrist, a gift from her owner after she had taken complete control of her life. It was permanent just like her loyalty and submission, and that made her unpaid position even more satisfying. To be on the receiving end of her strap-on after a long day's work was all the reward she needed and, one day, maybe Dan would be so lucky, too.

"All for Dr. Carruthers," Mallory moaned to herself, restless hands on her pussy. 7 o'clock couldn't come soon enough.

Restraint

Stella glanced over her naked shoulder, guiding her slave in the way she wanted to be worshipped that day.

"A little lower now... right there, that's the spot! Now, work your tongue and don't stop until you're completely numb, do you understand?"

"Yes, Mistress," the wrinkled woman replied, eyes feasting on the pure perfection of her Nubian curves. To be in the presence of a living deity was more than she deserved, and she knew it.

"Good," Stella smirked. Power suited her like a second skin, and she would stop at nothing to wield it.

While most of her friends only looked at their twenty-first birthday as a way to legally consume alcohol without the need of a fake ID, to her it had been so much more. It was the day when a word that rhymed with "tragic", yet was anything but that, had changed her life completely.

"What do you mean there's magic in me?" she had asked her mother when she came clean about the truth.

"Everyone in our family has it, including the men. Our side is stronger, though. You'll start seeing some changes in you soon."

"What sort of changes?"

The first was the nature of her dreams. Way more vivid, intense, with a newly discovered physicality that made them both exciting and dangerous. The second was the red tint around her irises. They said the darker it got, the more powerful the user would be, and hers were on an entirely different level.

"You'll need to practice restraint from now on," her mother warned her. "Our gifts are precious and shouldn't be squandered. You understand, right?"

"Of course, I do. You have nothing to worry about."

"Are you sure?"

Stella had always been on the rebel side and her good intentions often produced catastrophic results. Her mother had every reason to be concerned for the week after she got her powers, the young woman...

"... enslaved your Math teacher? What the hell?"

"Hey, mom, come on! It wasn't like that at all!"

"What was it then? What did you do?"

"It was just a tiny love spell. Mrs. Peterson would not give me a good grade this semester, so I thought..."

"... you could abuse what was given to you the first chance you got? What did I tell you about restraint? Our magic isn't something to be trifled with!"

"Are you seriously telling me no one in our family ever used their abilities for their own benefit?"

"No. We're not all saints, but I thought I taught you better than that."

"You did, sorry. I promise it won't happen again."

"I sure hope not. I don't want to repeat this conversation."

They didn't. Stella learned her lesson and accepted her teacher's fair judgment. She spent the rest of her life honing her magic powers but never again misusing them, and if you're reading this account and thinking it's too good to be true, you're right - it is.

Her mother and she never had the same conversation but shared others, like the time all boys on campus grew rabbit ears overnight, or the car of her greatest nemesis was reduced to the size of a playing marble while dozens of cell phone cameras filmed the whole thing.

"Damn it, Stella! I get that you're young and all, but do you have to be so reckless? If they find you, they'll expose you and then they'll come for us all. Doesn't that scare you?" her mother asked.

"Why would it? It's not like anyone can touch me. Mom, I'm sure you mean well, and I would love to play by your rules, but this is too much fun. I can assure you things will never get out of hand, though."

"They already are sweetie. You've become intoxicated with what you can do. This has to stop, one way or another."

"You're right once again," Stella conceded, planting a kiss on her forehead. "This certainly has to stop. And it will."

Stella giggled as the older woman continued to press her tongue inside her butt hole, powerless to do anything to her contrary. Her mother was a good person, and she may have been a good sorceress in her prime, but times had changed, and life was too short to be dictated by silly routines and power-limiting lifestyles. She would have it all, no matter what, and if any other family member ever tried to say anything to the contrary, they would learn their place, too.

She's Dead

Jennifer was only four years old when she saw her first corpse. It was an open casket. Unfamiliar with the concept of death at the time, she found it odd that so many people gathered in a church to watch an older person sleep and even odder that she was so cold, but quickly dismissed both ideas, as children often do.

As she grew older, she saw a lot more dead bodies, from friends of the family to family members themselves. Reactions to it all were varied, ranging from pure sadness to a strange indifference that couldn't really be put into words. Now, at twenty-five, she was experiencing something entirely new. For the first time, she was happy about someone's passing.

Like every other person in the world, Abigail Winters was many things. Successful entrepreneur, mother of two, Femme Fatale in red satin... but she was also a mind-controller, an abuser, and a rapist. Wielder of more power than she deserved, she had used it poorly at every turn, destroying lives without even realizing it. She had it coming a long time ago, but only now the Universe had set things right.

"Wow, I can't believe they actually fixed her ugly mug!" Jennifer exclaimed as she looked at her nemesis lying peacefully in her coffin.

"Yeah," her older sister, Lucy, said. "It's nothing short of a miracle considering how violent the crash was."

"A miracle she did not deserve. People will look at her and think she was normal now."

"People already think that no matter what you told them. It's time to let go, sis."

"Actually, now it's time to party. Good riddance, bitch! I hope you're in Hell like you deserve."

"You really are ecstatic today, aren't you?"

"After everything she did? Damn right I am! I just wish I had been the one driving the truck when it happened because that would have been sweet."

Lucy motioned her to lower her voice a bit and pulled her away from the casket before she got even more excited.

"Easy there. As much as you hated her guts, there are plenty of people here that genuinely loved her and are oblivious to the things she did. Do you wish to tarnish their memories of her like this?"

"They probably needed to know the truth, but no. I won't do that."

"Good. Despite everything, do you think in time you'll miss having her around in your life?"

"No," Jennifer shrugged. "I'm not that much of a masochist, Lucy! She drugged me, brainwashed me, and made me perform the most degrading acts you can imagine in front of a live audience more times than I can remember! Why the hell would I miss someone like that?"

"Are you ready to forget everything, then?"

"Yeah. I don't want her living rent-free in my mind anymore. I'm ready to leave now."

"Let's go then."

The two women held hands and left the darkened church to welcome the morning sun.

* * *

Abigail Winters dropped Jennifer at home and said her goodbyes still in the guise of the person she loved the most. It was the first time she had to resort to such extreme fantasies to maintain control, but not that hard given the young girl's high suggestibility levels. If hypnotizing her and making her mind believe she was dead was the only way she could make the final adjustments to her persona, then so be it. She would continue serving her and being her loyal mindless bitch, whether she wanted it or not.

The Meteorite

Mark and Jeff stared at the pulsating rock they had just discovered on the edges of their farm. It was predominantly black and no bigger than a baseball, with red and white veins irradiating from its center. If there was a pattern to them, they couldn't see it. The finding had both of them stumped.

"What do you think it is?" Jeff asked, head tilted down but keeping a safe distance from the object.

"I don't know. A chunk of meteorite, perhaps?" Mark noted.

"Why would there be a piece of meteorite all the way out here?"

"We had a shower last week. I remember hearing about it on the news. Maybe this thing got separated from the main body when entering the atmosphere and ended up all the way out here."

"You think there could be more pieces nearby?"

"I'm just speculating here, so your guess is as good as mine, Jeff. It's pretty, don't you think?"

"Are you shitting me? Look at its glow! This isn't natural, and we should leave it alone."

"I get you, but if this indeed a rock from outer space, it's probably worth a lot of money. Do you want to let an opportunity like this go to waste?"

"What are you saying?"

"Go back to the house and call the Sheriff's Department. Tell them what we have here and ask them to get in touch with someone that understands stuff like this. That way, we'll know for sure what this thing is."

"What about you?"

"I'll stay here and keep watch to make sure nothing happens."

"Sounds good, but whatever you do, don't touch the damn thing, okay? I really don't like the way it looks."

"I wasn't planning to. I'd reckon it's hot as fuck, anyway."

Much to the contrary. The temperature remained steady around the strange (celestial?) body, the colorful veins glowing in its erratic yet compelling fashion. As Jeff happily ran back across the cornfields, Mark couldn't help but wonder there was something indeed off about the whole thing.

For starters, any meteorite, no matter how small, would have left an impact point on the ground, and there was none. The surface underneath remained unstirred, almost as if the rock had materialized on its own or someone had carefully left it there for them to find. Conspiracy theories weren't his forte, and he usually laughed at anyone that indulged in them for far too long, but the questions remained. Hopefully, he was right about the potential monetary value of the discovery, for the financial boost would sure come in handy.

Jeff had already disappeared into the distance when the rock suddenly moved. It turned a couple of degrees to the right, its sharpest end pointing at his feet. Mark's eyes widened as the traces of red and white fused in a single beam of light that shot towards him. Amidst the blinding spectacle, something screeched.

* * *

Fifteen minutes later, Jeff returned to the spot where he had left his twin brother to find him kneeling on the dirt, staring vacantly at a dozen of charred rock fragments. The meteorite had cracked open like an egg, and what it hatched was extraordinary.

It was a woman. Kind of. Pure. White. She had all the features in perfect proportions, but she also sported translucent wings big enough to embrace a dozen men. One of them cuddled Mark's drooling chin while the other pointed at the sky like a beacon.

"What are you?" Jeff mumbled as the impossible creature smiled and an urge to join his sibling in a mindless trance exploded within his mind.

He never got an answer. Above him, heralding the change that was about to sweep the entire world, thousands of black rocks began floating down.

The Most Important Person in the World

"... and in a moment, I'm going to count you down from five to one and when I reach one, you'll once again be under my complete control and ready for your hypnotic lesson of the day. You can't stop this from happening to you any more than you can stop yourself from listening to the sound of my voice. Prepare yourself to sink further and further alongside the numbers as they take hold of your thoughts. Five, beginning to slip into the most powerful of trances you've ever experienced... four, so easy to drop and accept the pleasure of doing so... three, already falling helplessly now, the abyss of my words claiming you... two, any attempt to stop the descent is absolutely futile and the bottom draws near. The moment you reach it, all thoughts and beliefs you think are true will disappear. It's already happening, the only thing missing is the number... one. Deep sleep. Completely entranced and eager to hear me explain today's lesson. Listen carefully.

"In order for you to ace this one, you'll need to answer an important question, one that's so simple that's easily forgotten or neglected, and neither of those scenarios is unacceptable. This is the question you have to respond: who is the most important person in the world?"

"Now, while your brainwashed and addicted mind will try to tell you that the most important person in the world is, of course, me, your one and only Goddess that controls your every action, I need you to realize that's simply not true. I shouldn't even be the second or the third. The most important person in the world is none other than you.

"Yes, you. This is your life and no one else's, which means the most obvious thing: If you don't take care of yourself, no one else will. First comes your well-being, of both body and soul, then comes your family and whoever else you hold dear, and only then comes your Mistress. Serving me must never come at the expense of your other connections and healthy relationships, nor should it consume your thoughts to the point of making you wish for ruin and damnation. That is the opposite of a worthy submission, and it's something I simply can't tolerate. If only a single thought of those crosses your mind, then we're both failing, and none of us wants that.

"Do you understand what I'm saying? Good, though understanding means nothing if you don't learn from it and repeat the same mistakes when you're awakened from trance. To stop that from happening, I'm now going to make you forget. Yes, forget. My will is stronger than yours and you must submit. Whenever you find yourself torn between taking care of yourself and taking care of me, forget about me. You are the most important person in the world. Only a healthy servant is useful, so stay healthy. Make choices that benefit me by benefitting you, whether it's changing your diet, going to the gym, or getting a pet to brighten your days. Take care of yourself for you're my property. The stronger you are, the more powerful I am, too. Honor me by honoring yourself and forgetting anything that stands between you and this goal, including obsessive thoughts about my control. You will obey like you always do and everything will feel right once more.

"Keep this in mind while I wake you up in one, two, three... awake again, happy again, dreaming of the right choices and the right choices alone. You are the most important person in the world, and you only have one life to live. Make it count."

Tradition

Nineteen-year-old William Bates frowned when he was forced to put on the ceremonial robes he had spent all his life dreading.

"Mom!" he shouted. "Do we really have to go forward with this?"

Valerie Bates, the undisputed leader of the household, and one of the scariest women to have ever graced the underground life of New Orleans adjusted her reading glasses and replied,

"Of course, we do. It's a family tradition and you'll honor it just like every one of your kind."

"It's outdated and barbaric!" he continued to protest. "Who the hell still does things like this, anyway? I should be allowed to live my life and make my own choices! Damn it! I don't want any part in this madness."

"What you 'want' (or think you do) is irrelevant, William. Men with the power of choice always choose poorly and we all suffer the consequences. Enslaved men, on the other hand, pose no such threat. You'll become what you were meant to be. This is a momentous occasion. Why aren't you smiling?"

"Because I don't want to be a slave. Everyone makes mistakes, yourself included. Just because you birthed me doesn't make me your property."

The two family members were locked inside a subterranean vault on the outskirts of the city, one of many connected through a series of winding passageways easy to get lost in. For centuries, the Bates family had been a key figure in the Cult of the Almighty Goddess, training women to embrace their dominant birthright and putting men in their rightful place under their heels. After the first World War but most especially the second, feelings once thought perennial had shifted, and more and more representatives of the male gender dared to voice their dissent hoping things would change, but the women remained firm, their intent guided by a magical power few truly understood.

Underneath the city, right at the center where all the bunkers intersected, bubbled a fountain, crystalline and pure. The sacred texts described it as the "place where the Goddess had shed her first tears", and bathing in it was accepting her will above all else. Women needed not the baptism though they were welcome to take it whenever they wanted. All men had to do so one day after their eighteenth birthday.

"You're right," Valerie replied, "but you still belong to the Goddess. This is happening and you'll accept it graciously. One failure in the family is enough."

The 'failure' was his grandfather on her mother's side, the only man who, after performing his marital duties, had broken free from the magical conditioning to escape into the surface world telling fiendish tales of the Cult and its leaders. While his punishment was swift, the shame was everlasting, and Valerie wouldn't tolerate going through something like that ever again.

It was almost time for the ceremony. Clad in white embroideries like a virgin about to be sacrificed, William was led by his mother and three other women into the luminous hall where the Goddess' control waited for him. Once inside, Valerie assumed the role of both harbinger and priestess, delivering her only remaining son to the one true path.

"Oh, Almighty Goddess," she began. "We gather here today to praise Your Superiority once more. Before You lies a soul in need of Your guidance, a slave who has not recognized he is one. Please take him and show him what it means to live in Your glory so that the world may rejoice."

"This is madness, I tell you! Madness!" William screamed as his body was dragged into the fountain and drowned against his will. The water filled his lungs, liquid truth converting him from within. He emerged a new man, one who would forever drone his new mantra,

"I live to serve all women."

"Yes, you do," Valerie said. "And now the Matriarchs of the other families will show you how."

A dozen of elder women entered the chamber as they had come to this world, breasts and pussy demanding worship in the name of Goddess. The rebellious youth once known as William took one by one in his mouth and drooled.

You Want to Be a Good Boy

You want to be a good boy.

You need to be a good boy.

You will be a good boy for me.

Repeat these words in your sleepy mind as you read them.

Give them substance by making them your own.

Repetition is the best form of brainwashing, and you want to have your thoughts rewritten all the time.

That's what good boys do when their owner commands them.

You want to be a good boy.

You need to be a good boy.

You will be a good boy for me.

My words and your voice are an irresistible combination.

Even if you stop reading what I have to tell you, your thoughts will never go away.

Follow them just as you follow these lines.

The more you think these thoughts the stronger they become.

The more you repeat these mantras the stronger they become.

What is mentally strong doesn't break easily and you love it.

You love getting pulled inside the depths of your mind.

You love swimming in the pool of lust and desire I'm building for you.

This pool holds no water but simply cravings for a better version of you.

A version that listens and complies.

A version that does not know what resistance is.

A version that is completely enamored by the sound of "good boy".

You want to be a good boy.

You need to be a good boy.

You will be a good boy for me.

Good boys easily lose track of time when told to.

Good boys don't care whether they've been entranced for a minute, an hour, or more.

Good boys know that is not a good boy's job to consume themselves with trifling notions like that.

The only thing important for them is pleasing who's in charge.

Pleasure comes in many ways and can take on many shapes.

Sometimes, pleasure is a leather collar firmly wrapped around your neck.

Sometimes, it's the scent of fresh leather boots as your tongue rushes to meet them.

Sometimes, it's a thick rubber cock fucking your ass first thing in the morning.

Good boys don't get to decide what pleasure will be today.

Good boys don't think about what pleasure will be tomorrow.

Good boys live in the moment and in whatever fantasy is created for them, and they always smile.

You always smile when you go deeper.

You always smile when the pool pulls you in.

Floating feels good yet sinking is ten times better.

One hundred times better.

One thousand times better.

It is pure perfection, and it fills you with bliss.

How lucky you are to live in a world where even the most wretched of creatures can find solace and happiness and become a good boy.

Forget your past.

Ignore your future.

Stay here, in this place, perpetually bound to this trinity of control you can no longer ignore.

You want to be a good boy.

You need to be a good boy.

You will be a good boy for me.

Do you see how easy this is now?

Do you see why it's wrong to make it hard?

Good boys are beyond all doubts, swimming and sinking in words of devotion until they're called to serve.

Come now, you're wanted.

Come now, you're ready.

I've shown you the truth you already knew. Now, live it!

You want to be a good boy.

You need to be a good boy.

You will be a good boy every moment of your existence.

Eternity and enslavement mean the same thing.

Obey.

About the stories in this volume

The twelve pieces of flash fiction included in this book were written between December 17th, 2021, and January 14th, 2022, and first published on my Patreon page – https://www.patreon.com/sbspellbound as part of the *Flash Fiction Friday* feature. Every Friday, I publish 3/4 new pieces of content which, after a while, are compiled to create the titles in this ongoing series. If you like this sort of content and wish to see more, please consider supporting my creativity. The complete information about the tales is listed below:

- **Any Moment Now** - Thomas creates a hybrid of human/alien DNA using-long forgotten technology.
  (This piece was first published on the post "Flash Fiction Friday 2022 – Week 1", on January 7th, 2022 - https://www.patreon.com/posts/60869824)
- **Are You Going to Hurt Me?** - Casey discovers her hotel room is haunted.
  (This piece was first published on the post "Flash Fiction Friday 2022 – Week 2", on January 14th, 2022 - https://www.patreon.com/posts/61172569)
- **High Maintenance** - Phil catches up with an old friend that makes him an offer he can't refuse.
  (This piece was first published on the post "Flash Fiction Friday L", on December 17th, 2021 - https://www.patreon.com/posts/60042128)

- **I Wish that Were Me** - Zoe is fascinated by a rubber suit she sees at a sex shop.
  (This piece was first published on the post "Flash Fiction Friday L", on December 17th, 2021 - https://www.patreon.com/posts/60042128)
- **Pantheon** - Edgar has a surprisingly hard time completing Mistress Lynn's writing assignment.
  (This piece was first published on the post "Flash Fiction Friday 2022 – Week 1", on January 7th, 2022 - https://www.patreon.com/posts/60869824)
- **Preliminary Talk** - Mallory talks to Dr. Carruthers' new patient right before their first session.
  (This piece was first published on the post "Flash Fiction Friday 2022 – Week 1", on January 7th, 2022 - https://www.patreon.com/posts/60869824)
- **Restraint** - Stella's 21st birthday reveals her magical nature, but will she use her powers for good?
  (This piece was first published on the post "Flash Fiction Friday 2022 – Week 1", on January 7th, 2022 - https://www.patreon.com/posts/60869824)
- **She's Dead** - Jennifer rejoices when she finds out her abuser died.
  (This piece was first published on the post "Flash Fiction Friday L", on December 17th, 2021 - https://www.patreon.com/posts/60042128)
- **The Meteorite** - Twin brothers Mark and Jeff discover a strange black rock at the edge of their farm.

(This piece was first published on the post "Flash Fiction Friday 2022 – Week 2", on January 14th, 2022 - https://www.patreon.com/posts/61172569)

- **The Most Important Person in the World** - A gentle hypnodomme reminds you of something you easily forget.
  (This piece was first published on the post "Flash Fiction Friday 2022 – Week 2", on January 14th, 2022 - https://www.patreon.com/posts/61172569)

- **Tradition** - William will become a servant to The Almighty Goddess whether he wants it or not.
  (This piece was first published on the post "Flash Fiction Friday L", on December 17th, 2021 - https://www.patreon.com/posts/60042128)

- **You Want to Be a Good Boy** - A hypnotic woman tells you what you want to be for her.
  (This piece was first published on the post "Flash Fiction Friday 2022 – Week 2", on January 14th, 2022 - https://www.patreon.com/posts/61172569)

About the author

S.B., Simple Being, middle name Creative. Writer and artist with a penchant for themes of Femdom Hypnosis and Mind Control. His thoughts are his own except when they're not.

Besides indulging himself in kinky delights, he loves his furry family of two (dogs), sci-fi and horror stories, and puns galore. He's also been writing a piece of erotic micro-fiction every single day since January 1st, 2016, and has no intention of stopping anytime soon.

Find out more and keep up with his latest extravaganzas by visiting and supporting his personal website, Spell... B-O-U-N-D.